Sabine Baring-Gould

English minstrelsie

a national monument of English song

Sabine Baring-Gould

English minstrelsie
a national monument of English song

ISBN/EAN: 9783741149993

Manufactured in Europe, USA, Canada, Australia, Japa

Cover: Foto ©Andreas Hilbeck / pixelio.de

Manufactured and distributed by brebook publishing software
(www.brebook.com)

Sabine Baring-Gould

English minstrelsie

ENGLISH MINSTRELSIE

English Minstrelsie

A National Monument of English Song

COLLATED AND EDITED, WITH NOTES AND
HISTORICAL INTRODUCTIONS, BY

S. BARING-GOULD, M.A.

THE AIRS, IN BOTH NOTATIONS, ARRANGED BY

H. FLEETWOOD SHEPPARD, M.A.

F. W. BUSSELL, B.D., Mus. B. Oxon.; AND

W. H. HOPKINSON, A.R.C.O.

IN EIGHT VOLUMES

VOLUME THE FOURTH

Edinburgh

T. C. & E. C. JACK, GRANGE PUBLISHING WORKS

1896

Printed by BALLANTYNE, HANSON & CO.
At the Ballantyne Press

NOTES TO SONGS

VOL. IV.

Tell me, Mary, how to Woo Thee (p. 1).—A song by C. A. Hodson, the words by F. Morrison. Hodson was the author of other favourite songs, as "Give me but my Arab Steed" and "My Home, my Happy Home."

The Pilgrim of Love (p. 6).—A favourite tenor song, the words by Mrs. Opie, and the music by Sir Henry R. Bishop. It was sung in "The Noble Outlaw," a ballad opera produced in 1815. Alfred Bunn says of Bishop's music at a later stage (in 1838): "If he will but be *himself*, the stuff is still in Bishop; but trying first to be Rossini, and after that to be Weber, knocked it all out of him. The composer of 'When the Wind Blows,' and the 'Chough and Crow,' and 'The Indian Drum,' and 'Mynheer Van Dunk' cannot afford to copy any one. Bishop has a classical and gentlemanly mind, which is as rare as it is pleasant to meet with in any one whose back has once rubbed against the scenes of a theatre."

How, O How, I needs must Part (p. 10).—John Dowland, the composer, was born in 1562, and at the age of twenty-six took his degree as Bachelor of Music. Anthony Wood says of him, that "he was the rarest musician that this age did behold." And Shakespeare has thus immortalised him in one of his sonnets—

> "If music and sweet poetry agree,
>   As they needs must (the sister and the brother),
> Then must the love be great 'twixt thee and me,
>   Because thou lov'st the one, and I the other.
> Dowland to thee is dear, whose heavenly touch
>   Upon the lute doth ravish human sense;
> Spenser to me, whose deep conceit is such,
>   As passing all conceit, needs no defence;
> Thou lov'st to hear the sweet melodious sound
>   That Phœbus' lute (the queen of music) makes,
> And I, in deep delight am chiefly drown'd
>   When as himself to singing he betakes.
> Our God is good to both, as poets feign,
> One knight loves both, and both in these remain."

Dowland travelled a good deal in Germany, France, and Italy. He is believed to have died in 1626 in Denmark. It is as a madrigal writer that this delightful musician made his principal mark.

The Deep, Deep Sea (p. 12).—A robust and fine song, by Horn.

Old Tubal Cain (p. 18).—The best of Henry Russell's songs. The words by Dr. C. Mackay.

Quaff with me the Purple Wine (p. 21).—A drinking-song, of which Shield is the composer. English song-books abound in "drinking songs;" some of the best verses in our language, and best tunes, are in honour of drink. The fashion of sitting at table, after the ladies had withdrawn, and singing bacchanalian songs, and tossing off glass after glass, has passed away for ever. Consequently these drinking-songs are gone, and few care now to sing them. Nevertheless, as a reminiscence of a stage of English social life, it is proper to give some of them.

Munden, in his "Memoirs," says, "The first £100 he realised he laid out in a pipe of port wine. At that time—the end of last century—a host would have blushed at his own want of hospitality had he sent away his guests sober. He hid their hats, locked the doors, and detained them by force. Austin once dined at the house of Mr. Bowes, who carried off Lady Strathmore. Being a domesticated man, he was desirous of quitting at a reasonable time. After earnestly remonstrating against the violence used to detain him, he at length lost patience, took up a plate, threw it at a pier-glass, which was smashed to pieces, exclaiming, 'Now, will you let me go?' His host, seeing him cast a menacing look at another in the room, threw down the key of the door, and called out, 'Oh! by G——, Austin, go as soon as you like.'"

The Girl I Left Behind Me (p. 26).—The late Mr. William Chappell says of the air of this favourite song, "that a manuscript copy of it of the date of 1770 was in the possession of Dr. Rimbault." He attributes the words to the date 1758 or 1759, when there were encampments on the Brighton Downs, whilst Admirals Hawke and Rodney were watching the French fleet in Brest harbour.

The air was appropriated by Moore for one of his "Irish Melodies," but there is no evidence that it is other than English in origin. The tune has been played for the last century as a loth-to-depart, when a man-of-war weighs anchor, and when a regiment quits the town in which it has been quartered; consequently it has been carried wherever English soldiers and mariners go.

Hearts of Oak (p. 28).—Boswell, in the account of his visit to Corsica, says that the Corsicans requested him to sing to them an English song, and thereupon he sang "Hearts of Oak." "Never did I see men so delighted with a song as the Corsicans were with 'Hearts of Oak.' '*Cuore di querco*,' cried they. '*Bravo, Inglesi!*' It was quite a joyous riot. I fancied myself to be a recruiting sea-officer. I fancied all my chorus of Corsicans aboard the British fleet." That was in 1765, or shortly after; Boswell published his book in 1768.

The words of this popular song were by David Garrick, and it acquired a run through having been sung by Champnes in "Harlequin's Invasion," in 1759. The tune was by Mr. (afterwards Dr.) Boyce. The song was introduced by Dr. Arnold into his opera, "The Genius of Nonsense," 1784. This song and air were born the same year as "The Girl I Left Behind Me," given in this volume. The year was a memorable one. The French had threatened an invasion, and made preparations in Havre, Toulon, and other ports; but in July, Rodney bombarded Havre, and did much damage to the town, destroying many of the flat-bottomed boats built as transports for troops. Admiral Boscawen also dispersed the Toulon fleet off Lagos. Another fleet under Hawke blockaded Brest, and he gained a signal victory near Quiberon over a French fleet in November.

A curious story is told by Parke in his "Musical Memoirs" relative to Dr. Boyce and his son. Some twenty years or more after the death of Dr. Boyce—he died in 1779—his son received a letter by post from an unknown person, requesting him to call on the writer immediately, as he had an important communication to make to him relative to his late father. Mr. Boyce repaired to the address given, which was in an obscure and dirty court in St. Giles. When he arrived there he inquired of the people of the house for the person of whom he was in quest, and was shown up three pairs of stairs to a back room; on entering which he found an old man in a squalid and wretched room, lying on a miserable bed, and apparently in a condition of extreme exhaustion. The old man, however, addressed him:—"Sir, I have been a beggar all my life, and during your good father's time my station was in the street in which he lived; and so kind and liberal was he to me, that few days passed without my receiving some charity as well as gracious words from him. I am now on my deathbed, and would like to bequeath to you my savings, as I have no relatives." Mr. Boyce was much surprised, but still more so when the dying beggar put into his hand a parcel of upwards of two thousand pounds in bank-notes.

𝖂𝖎𝖙𝖍 𝕷𝖔𝖂𝖋𝖞 𝕾𝖚𝖎𝖙 𝖆𝖓𝖉 𝕻𝖑𝖆𝖎𝖓𝖙𝖎𝖁𝖊 𝕯𝖎𝖙𝖙𝖞 (p. 30).—

From "No Song, no Supper," Storace, as usual, borrowed for the setting of the songs in this pleasant little piece; two are from the French, but this song was taken from the chant of a blind beggar in the streets, with, of course, some polish given to it. It was sung with great effect by Signora Storace.

In John Bannister's Memoirs is an account of the first appearance of 'No Song, no Supper," in 1789:—

"This piece, supported by the united talents of Kelly, Dignum, Suett, Bannister, Mrs. Crouch, Storace, and Romanzini, was received with cordial approbation, was often repeated, and for many years a constant favourite. Every part was most judiciously adapted to the powers and appearance of the performers; not a syllable, not a note, was uttered in vain. In the incidents—for a plot can hardly be ascribed to it—there is nothing new: the old story of John Blunt and his wife, who will not bolt the outward door, but leave it to be done by the party who shall first break silence; an honest farmer whose patience and purse are exhausted by a knavish attorney; the pettifogger coming in his absence, to sup, at least, with his wife, and driven to take refuge in a flour-sack; the discovery and exposure of the hidden supper and the concealed lawyer by means of a song of Storace, which was never to be sung before a poor feast— all these things, if soberly related or seriously discussed, would seem hardly worthy of consideration, but with the aid of agreeable music and exquisite acting, the objections of criticism were over-ruled or suppressed, and 'No Song, no Supper,' was in the highest degree popular."*

Parke, in his "Musical Memoirs," confirms what Bannister says, that "the melody was taken from an old street ditty." He adds that "Signora Storace in this ballad was unanimously encored."

Indeed, she made a great hit with this song. Nancy Storace was the sister of Stephen Storace. Her real Christian names were Anne Selina. She was born in 1765, and was two years younger than her gifted brother. Nancy was trained as a singer, and had a decided taste for music. She sang at Florence in 1780. There was an unpleasant harshness in her countenance, and her figure was clumsy, and there was some coarseness in her voice, that unfitted her for serious opera, and she was at her best in comic opera. In Italy she came to know Michael Kelly, then just emerging from boyhood, and was very kind to him. She was engaged at Vienna at the same time that he was, and once paid his gambling debts. Kelly speaks of her as good-hearted and generous in the extreme. Whilst she was at Vienna she married a violin-player called

*The main plot, with the song that produces the supper, was taken from a mediæval Fabliau of the 13th century, given in Méon, i. p. 104, and in modern French by Le Grand d'Aussy, iv. p. 55. Prince Hoare, who wrote the play, did not take the plot directly thence, but from the French comic opera, "Le soldat magicien," based on the ancient tale.

Fisher, a very eccentric man, an inordinate talker, and very ugly.

Scarcely was she married before she repented her rashness. She and her spouse spent their leisure in fighting—literally, not figuratively; and when she was suffering from a black eye, the Emperor Joseph ordered the bullying fiddler off from his capital, and he departed for Ireland.

In 1787 she repaired to London, and at once was engaged for the King's Theatre, and for the Ancient Concerts. She was a good and lively actress, with plenty of arch humour, but her manner was a little vulgar. After the death of her brother in 1796, Nancy Storace left England and visited Paris and Italy. After four years of this wandering life she returned to London, and sang in "The Cabinet," by Tom Dibdin, and in "The Siege of Belgrade." She quitted the stage in 1808, as she became aware that her voice was failing. On the 30th of May she appeared for the last time in her favourite part of Margaretta in "No Song, no Supper," and sang this pleasant street ditty, "With Lowly Suit." Colman wrote for her a farewell address of about a dozen lines, which she sang, but her emotion was visibly perceptible, and was more than her strength could bear. When she reached the line, "Farewell, and bless you all for ever!" she was so overcome by her feelings that she fainted, and was carried off the stage insensible.

In her private life she was universally respected. Seven years after her retirement, Signora Storace was dining with her old friend Kelly, when she was seized with a shivering fit, and complained of being ill. A few days after she was dead, at the comparatively early age of forty-nine.

In the play, "No Song, no Supper," a sham meal is never brought on. A steaming hot boiled leg of lamb and turnips may be described as quite the leading character in the entertainment. Without this appetising addition the play has never been represented.

𝕮𝖊𝖑𝖊𝕭𝖗𝖆𝖙𝖊 𝖙𝖍𝖎𝖘 𝕱𝖊𝖘𝖙𝖎𝕭𝖆𝖑 (p. 33).—

One of the birthday odes to Queen Mary, composed by Henry Purcell. It is in this song that the absurd incongruity exists of making the voice imitate a flourish of trumpets to the line, "Bid the Trumpets Cease."

Mary was born April 30, 1662. The year when William was away from England on her birthday, engaged in an unsuccessful campaign in Flanders, was 1692. In June he lost Namur, and was defeated with great loss in August at Steinkirk.

𝕿𝖍𝖊 𝕽𝖔𝖘𝖊 𝖙𝖍𝖆𝖙 𝖂𝖊𝖊𝖕𝖘 (p. 36).—

A song by Mrs. Radcliffe that occurs in her "Romance of the Forest." It is thus introduced—the style is characteristic of the authoress and of her time:—"The contrast which memory gave of the past with the present drew tears of tenderness and gratitude to their eyes, and the sweet smile which seemed struggling to dispel from the countenance of Adeline those gems of sorrow, penetrated the heart of Theodore. He took up a lute that lay on the table, and, touching the dulcet chords, accompanied it with the following words." William Horsley was born in London in 1774, and died 1858. "The Rose that Weeps" was produced in 1798 or the following year.

𝕴𝖓 𝖙𝖍𝖎𝖘 𝕺𝖑𝖉 𝕮𝖍𝖆𝖎𝖗 (p. 38).—

A song from Balfe's opera of "The Maid of Honour," the words by Fitzball. Fitzball says: "Balfe told me, not long ago, that he always considered 'The Maid of Honour' his most finished performance. He is, or ought to be, the best judge of that, although we are very few of us best judges of ourselves. The public seemed mightily pleased with this new opera; the plot, in particular, was exceedingly amusing. 'We come when you ring the bell' and the 'Arm-Chair' were gems of admirable setting. Mr. Sims Reeves never played or sang better than in the young farmer, which he looked to perfection; when he loses his mind, how truthful he was to character! The house melted into tears while he so touchingly poured forth, from the deepest recesses of his heart, that popular cavatina, ' In this Old Chair my Father Sat.' "

Signor Balfi-

THACKERAY'S SKETCH OF BALFE.

(From Planché's " Recollections and Reflections.")

Nevertheless " The Maid of Honour " failed, and the reason is given by Planché in his " Recollections and Reflections."

In the season 1846–47 " Lucia di Lammermoor " was produced at Drury Lane by Jullien. It took the town by surprise, and the receipts averaged £400 nightly, and the opera would have run through the season. But Jullien was bound to produce a new opera by Balfe before Christmas or forfeit £200, and this new opera was " The Maid of Honour." It was madness whilst " Lucia " was in full swing of popular favour to give it up for Balfe's opera. Planché says : " Forrester and I had entreated Jullien to pay the forfeit, if Balfe insisted on it, and not to take ' Lucia ' out of the bills while its attraction was undiminished. But no ; he would not be advised. He would not even appeal to Balfe, who, in the face of the facts, might have consented to waive or reduce the penalty and permit the postponement of his opera until novelty was required." The result was, of course, that " The Maid of Honour " failed ; the salaries could not be paid, the theatre was closed, and Jullien became a bankrupt.

Meet Me By Moonlight (p. 40).—Joseph Augustine Wade, the composer of this favourite song, was born in Dublin at the close of the last or beginning of the present century, the son of a dairyman. He found employment in the Record Office in Dublin, but his restless disposition induced him to migrate to London, where he was engaged by the firm of Chappell to make himself generally useful, but his intemperate habits and want of application necessitated his dismissal. He was president or chairman of a club or society called the " Owls," comprising many choice spirits, but all addicted to the bottle. The Rev. J. Richardson thus describes him :— " He was a wise man in theory, and a fool in practice. A vigorous intellect swathed in the trammels of insuperable indolence ; planning everything, performing nothing. Always in difficulties, having the

means at hand to extricate himself from their annoyance, yet too apathetic to arouse himself to an effort ; content to dream away his time in any occupation but that which the requisitions of the occasion demanded. Surrounded with books of all sorts ; extracting portions of each, and jumbling the several parts into a mass, which he could neither digest nor comprehend ; amusing himself with all kinds of musical instruments, and rejecting all the amusements they afforded ; increasing the confusion of his brain by repeated potations of any fluid which at the moment might be before him, appearing, even in this practice, to have no choice or predilection.

" This man, reduced by his follies and his indolence to the drudgery of writing musical critiques for obscure publications, and delivering his opinions as the stipendiary oracle of a publisher of music, was, a few years before his death, received into the family of a M. Anati, who, having held a military commission under Murat, King of Naples, and left Italy after the death of his master, obtained the appointment of professor of foreign languages at the college of Winchester. Wade was employed by Anati to instruct his daughter in the science of thorough bass, counterpoint, &c., and for so doing received a handsome salary. He left London for Winchester to enter upon his duties by the railway train, unencumbered with luggage, and not overburdened with money, and arrived at his journey's end shortly before the dinner hour of his employer. His external appearance was the contrary to a letter of recommendation ; his clothes were threadbare and dusty ; his linen and face unwashed, and bilious.

" The good nature of the host looked over these little aberrations from decorum, and on his informing him that he had inadvertently left London without his portmanteau, very kindly supplied him with a temporary outfit from his own wardrobe, including a garment indispensable to everybody but a Highlander. Thus equipped he made his appearance at the dinner-table, and though the ladies thought there was something odd in him, his conversation and his manners soon reconciled them to his company.

" It cannot be said that during the twelvemonth that he remained in his new quarters he was very sedulous in the performance of the duty for which he was engaged. He, however, imparted valuable musical knowledge to his pupil."

Unhappily, the force of example operates on old as well as young, and Wade lured his host on to become a toper. They sat up together half the night, and almost every night, drinking gin and water, and talking of " man's weak, helpless state." At last the term of Wade's engagement hastened to an end, and he did not relish the idea of returning to make shift for a livelihood, and to pay for his potations. So one evening, over the gin and water, he said to his host, " By dad, Anati, it will be mighty uncomfortable for me to leave this house, so I'll e'en mak' shift and marry your daughter, and stay here *in sæcula sæculorum.*"

This was too much for the proud Neapolitan, and leaping from the table, he rushed to a cupboard, produced two pistols, threw one at the music-master, and said, " To death ! for this insult ! "

The musician, sobered instantly, instead of picking up the pistol offered him, scampered out of the room, fled the house, and returned on foot as fast as he could to London.

From this time his downward progress was rapid, and he died in London, July 15, 1845.

His song, " Meet Me by Moonlight Alone," was sung by Vestris, and became vastly popular, as did also his duet, " I've Wandered in Dreams." His song, " Meet Me by Moonlight," had the good fortune to be immortalised in the pages of *Frazer's Magazine* for October 1834 by the witty Father Prout, who rendered it very happily in French. Wade was associated with Macfarren as arranger of the earlier issues of Mr. W. Chappell's " National English Airs."

Through the Wood (p. 42).—By Horn, of whom something has already been said.

Tom Bowling (p. 48).—Another of Incledon's favourite songs. It is by Charles Dibdin, and was introduced by him into "The Oddities" at the Lyceum Theatre, 1789.

I have already given a sketch of poor Charles Incledon's life, and I promised some anecdotes about him. Several capital stories of Incledon are in the Memoirs of Charles Mathews.

The latter and Liston were one day in a shop in Bond Street, which was full of perfumery, toys, and nicknacks. They had been looking at some amulets of a black composition on which was stamped the head of George III. in commemoration of the jubilee, when Incledon entered the shop. Liston at once pointed out these amulets, and gravely told the vocalist that they were throat lozenges. Incledon was very fond of trying all kinds of quack medicines, and he at once bought one of these objects, though it cost him half-a-guinea. Liston told him that the lozenge must be kept in his mouth all day, although it was as large as a locket or a brooch. Away went the singer, quite taken in, stuffing the amulet into his mouth.

At night the greenroom party had been apprised of the jest, and agreed to assist in prolonging it. Incledon entered with his mouth distended with the lozenge, which he was still sucking, and assured the inquirers that it had done his voice great good. Mr. Kemble, who was present, advised the vocalist to complete the benefit by keeping it in his mouth all night.

"But my dear Mr. Kemble," he replied, "it may choke me in my sleep."

"Oh no," answered the great tragedian, "Mrs. Incledon can attend to you in the night, and pull it out if she finds you struggling with it."

Actually Incledon retired to bed sucking his amulet, and retained it in his mouth all night, but of course in consequence was unable to sleep.

Meanwhile Liston or Mathews had contrived to insert in the next day's paper a paragraph to the effect that Bonaparte, actuated by hatred against the English, had contrived a trinket in the form of a brooch, adorned with a miniature likeness of the king, which was impregnated with a subtle poison, that destroyed the coat of the throat and corroded the lungs, with the express object of getting it introduced into Great Britain so as to spoil the voices of the most eminent English singers. When Incledon read this paragraph he nearly fell seriously ill with fright, and the practical jokers were obliged to confess what they had done. Incledon was so good-natured that he at once forgave them.

In 1812 Incledon and Mathews were united in an entertainment wherewith they travelled the provinces. At Leicester, Incledon was to appear as Steady in "The Quaker," but finding no suitable set of garments in the theatrical wardrobe, he had the audacity to walk up to a respectable chemist in the town, who belonged to the Society of Friends, and ask him the loan of his hat, coat, breeches, and waistcoat for the evening. He had such a pleasant way that he actually got the old gentleman, to whom he was an absolute stranger, and who regarded all players as limbs of the devil, to fit him out with clothes for the evening performance.

In his later years, when the taste in music was altered, and ran in the direction of "Italianised humbug," as Incledon called it, and sea-songs were less cared for, the vocalist considered himself neglected by the nobility, who had once patronised him, and he became soured against persons of rank. One day a friend happening to quote some slighting remark on old English songs made by a nobleman, Incledon fired up and exclaimed, "D—— all lords!" then, suddenly, an idea crossed his brain that he had uttered an impious speech. He solemnly removed his hat, and looking upwards with devout earnestness, added in a low, tremulous voice, "except the Lord of lords."

"Poor Incledon," says Mrs. Mathews; "he had an expansive heart, but a defective education, and the example of early associations had somewhat depraved his manner of discourse." The evil of swearing upon all occasions was contracted by Incledon in early life, when a boy in the navy, it being also the vice of his day amongst people not highly bred, and, indeed, not altogether disdained in polite life. In later years, when such language became out of fashion, he was so confirmed in its use that he was not aware how offensive he was apt to be.

He was very absent at times. During a journey with Mathews in a stage-coach, he had been greatly annoyed with wasps, and although the journey was one of forty miles, Incledon was convinced that the same insect had travelled with the coach for the purpose of annoying him. He would exclaim, "There's that cursed wasp again!" trying, with many imprecations, to destroy it.

A grave, taciturn gentleman sitting opposite him in the coach, towards the end of the day, fell asleep. Incledon was still occupied in evading the wasp, when, to his delight, it settled on the nose of the sleeper. Incledon at once sprang up and struck with his fist on the insect, crying out, "Ha! d—— you, I've done for you now!" It may be imagined what effect this outrage had upon the unfortunate recipient, and it required all Incledon's asseverations, and some additional oaths, to convince the stranger that he had not really intended to do for him.

Mrs. Mathews says: "As a man of extraordinary vocal talent, he had been admired and petted, and his nature being self-indulgent, vain, and weak, he often acted as if he disregarded everything but his own wishes. In this he did himself an injustice, for he was a kind and liberal man, but he lived like a child all his life, and had been so spoiled by everybody about him, that his mind, by nature feeble, had no scope for enlargement. His character, in fact, never grew up, and he was as much a boy at sixty as at sixteen."

The Roast Beef of Old England (p. 50).—A famous song by Richard Leveridge, of whom an account has already been given. He was born in 1670, and died in great poverty in 1758. His voice remained unimpaired so long, that in 1730, when sixty years old, he offered, for a wager of a hundred guineas, to sing a bass song against any man in England. In 1727 he published his songs, with the music, in two small 8vo vols. Fielding has a song in his comedy of "Don Quixote in England," which appeared in 1733, that begins with the same verse as does Leveridge's, but has a second which is different; and this was sung to the air of "The Queen's Old Courtier." Leveridge's song appears in Walsh's "British Musical Miscellany," 1730, and of "The Universal Musician," circ. 1750. It appears also on an early undated half-sheet. Hogarth's famous picture of "O the Roast Beef of Old England, or the Gate of Calais," is the result of an expedition to Calais in 1747. The original picture was painted for Lord Charlemont. Soon after it was finished it accidentally fell, and a nail ran through the cross on the top of the gate. Hogarth endeavoured in vain to mend it with the same colour, so as to conceal the blemish; he therefore introduced a starved crow, looking down on the roast beef, and thus effectually covered the defect. The crow does not appear in the engravings of the picture. The artist was arrested whilst sketching the gate, and he was conducted before the Commandant, who overhauled both him and his sketches, but as he found only caricatures, and no drawings that showed he had been observing and planning the fortifications, he dismissed Hogarth, but ordered him back to his ship. In the picture he has represented himself in the corner making the sketch, and on his shoulder appears the hand of the musketeer who arrested him.

Many songs have been written to Leveridge's tune, one in praise of old English beer, and several anti-Jacobite songs; also one on the fable of "The Frog and the Ox," written by Hogarth's friend, Theophilus Forest, introduced into a metrical composition that describes Hogarth's picture:—

> "With lanthorn jaws and meagre cut,
> See how the half-starved Frenchmen strut,
> And call us English dogs.
> But soon we'll teach these bragging foes
> That *Beef* and *Beer* give heavier blows
> Than wine and roasted frogs."

In 1738 a French company was announced to give a series of performances at the Haymarket Theatre, "under distinguished patronage."

As it was publicly threatened that the performance would be violently interfered with, a detachment of soldiers was ordered to the Haymarket, and one of the Westminster magistrates, Justice Deveil, took a seat in the pit as representative of law and order. Nothing so exasperated John Bull in those days as to flourish the French flag before his eyes, for he was nothing if not national. As soon as possible after the doors were opened, the house was crammed from floor to ceiling, and the audience sounded the note of hostility by thundering in chorus Leveridge's "Roast Beef of Old England." When the curtain rose, the actors were discovered standing between two files of Grenadier Guards, the soldiers with fixed bayonets, and resting upon their firelocks. A roar of indignation greeted this sight; the whole pit rose, and turning to the Justice, demanded the withdrawal of the military. He was intimidated, and gave the order required. But the actors had no sooner opened their mouths than there rose a storm of cat-calls, hisses, howls, and snatches of "The Roast Beef of Old England;" and shouts were heard demanding how a parcel of French rascals dared come on English stages and oust our native performers.

In vain did the Justice endeavour to obtain order. The actors, unable to make their voices heard, ranged themselves for a dance; then from all parts of the house rained a hailstorm of peas, covering the stage and rendering dancing impossible. Justice Deveil shouted for a candle to read the Riot Act, and threatened to recall the military. This made the disturbance, if possible, greater. The French and Spanish ambassadors and their wives and suite, and other aristocratic patrons, escaped from the house, and the management lowered the curtain. By degrees the rioters dispersed, still roaring out snatches of their favourite song. "And," says a contemporary writer, "no battle gained by Marlborough ever elicited more frantic enthusiasm than did this victory over foreign actors."

Sfp, Sfp, pe Laзy Hours (p. 52).—A song by Eccles, a composer most unjustly neglected. He belongs to Purcell's school, and is only second to that great master. This was one of Mrs. Bracegirdle's songs. In the original there is but a single verse. Two more have been added.

Old Adam (p. 54).—This curious air was taken down from William Andrews, a fiddler at Sheepstor, on the edge of Dartmoor. I made two visits to the old man, one in 1890 with Mr. Sheppard, when we failed to extract much from him. I went again in 1892 with Mr. Bussell, and then his shyness was broken down, and we spent two hours with him, noting down his old airs. We might have got more, but the Rector most kindly came in and insisted on our going to tea with him. We could not refuse, and then had to

IV

hasten to catch our train to return, and as we passed, more than an hour after having left the old man, we heard him still fiddling. His memory was stored with old airs. As he told me, in ancient days when there were dances in the farm-houses, all the young folk sang as they danced, and the "burden" or refrain served to mark the turns in the dance. As he told me, he "minded his viddle more than them zingers;" consequently we could obtain the words in a fragmentary condition—rarely more than the first verse. The poor old fellow died last autumn, and there is an end to his music on earth. "Old Adam" was one of the songs of which he could recall but a scrap of words, and I have therefore been compelled to write new verses, following as far as I could the idea of the ancient song. The air is peculiar in character, and the metre unusual. One would like to know what was the dance performed to it.

When Daisies Pied (p. 56).—Shakespeare's delightful song in "Love's Labour's Lost," with the music by Arne, and worthy of the words; higher praise could not be given.

Love Lies Bleeding (p. 58).—An old English air, once very popular, contained in every copy of the "Dancing Master" from and after 1686; in Walsh's "Dancing Master" in "Pills to Purge Melancholy." A sort of parody on the song is "Law Lies Bleeding," and begins:—

> "Lay by your pleading, Law lies a-bleeding;
> Burn all your studies, and throw away your reading."

The original words are found in "Merry Drollery Complete," 1661 and 1670, but, according to Mr. Ebsworth, are before 1658 and after 1648; but there "Love Lies a-Bleeding" is said to be in imitation of "Law Lies a-Bleeding," which is probably an inversion of the fact. The tune is also called "The Cyclops." I have ventured in this instance to give a set of fresh words to the tune.

The original song is in ten stanzas. Of these I give the first two and last as a sample. Till Mr. Ebsworth reprinted "Merry Drollery Complete," it was supposed that the words of this air were lost:—

I.

> "Lay by your pleading,
> Love lies bleeding.
> Burn all your Poetry, and throw away your reading.
> Piety is painted,
> And Truth is tainted.
> Love is a reprobate, and Schism now is sainted.
> The Throne Love doth sit on
> We dayle do spit on;
> It was not thus, I wis, when *Betty* rul'd in *Britain*;
> But Friendship hath faultered,
> Love's altars are altered,
> And he that is the cause, I would his neck were halter'd.

2.

> "When Love did nourish,
> *England* did flourish,
> Till holy hate came in, and made us all so currish.
> Now every widgeon
> Talks of Religion,
> And doth as little good as Mahomet and his pidgeon.
> Each coxcombe is suiting
> His words for confuting,
> But heaven is sooner gain'd by suffering than disputing.
> True friendship we smother,
> And strike at our Brother,
> Apostles never went to God by killing one another.

B

10.

" Then let the Graces
Crown our embraces,
And let us settle all things in their proper places.
Lest persecution
Cause dissolution,
Let all purloyned wealth be made a restitution.
For though now it tickles,
'Twill turn all to prickles ;
Then let's live in peace, and turn our Swords to sickles.
When *Noah's* Dove was sent out,
Then God's Pardon went out :
They that would have it so, I hope will say Amen to it."

who had the pleasure of witnessing it, I think it impossible it can ever be forgotten. This piece was very productive to the treasury, at little or no expense. In it there was a ballad, written by Mr. M. G. Lewis, and composed by myself, which was sung by Miss Decamp, entitled ' No, my Love, No.' I believe I may say it was the most popular song of the day ; it was not alone to be found upon every pianoforte, but also to be heard in every street, for it was a great favourite with the ballad-singers."

This song was sung to me by the daughter of a taverner in a little village inn in Cornwall, so that it may be said still to hold its own.

Dr ARNE.

No, my Love, No. (p. 60).—A song from "Of Age To-morrow," a musical entertainment by Thomas Dibdin, based on one of Kotzebue's pieces. Michael Kelly wrote the music. It was acted with great success at Drury Lane in 1799. Tom Dibdin says in his Memoirs: " I wrote this farce to oblige Mr. Bannister. As I was *bonâ fide* in the employ of Mr. Harris at this time, I took no remuneration for that simple and successful piece, except three drawings, presented me by Mr. B. The farce was of German origin, and imported in that language by Mr. Papendick, one of his late Majesty's pages, who offered it to Mr. Harris. Mr. Harris declined it, and I was permitted to put it into its present form without being named as the author."

Kelly says in his Recollections: "This farce was, and is, a great favourite ; nothing could be more perfect than the acting and singing of Mrs. Charles Kemble, then Miss Decamp ; by those

The story of the origin of the successful play, "Of Age To-morrow," is told in the memoirs of John Bannister :—" Kotzebue, having written a farce, which he fancied might succeed in England as well as in Germany, forwarded it to his friend Mr. Papendick, one of her Majesty's pages, who made a translation and tendered it to Mr. Harris, by whom it was refused. He had also shown it to Bannister, who thought the incidents and situations might be produced with effect, and, accompanied by Kelly, went to Windsor, where they soon made an arrangement with Mr. Papendick, and acquired his right in the piece. At the request of Bannister, Tom Dibdin wrote the dialogue anew, and added some songs ; and one was contributed by Lewis. It was brought out (1st February) as ' Of Age To-morrow' with complete success. Miss De Camp supported it by her admirable acting, and by the exquisite style in which she sang the songs, particularly that of Lewis, 'O No, my

Love, No,' which immediately became a favourite with all classes. ' Of Age To-morrow ' was performed thirty-six times, and produced ample profit to Bannister, and to Kelly, who shared in the adventure and composed the music."

Prettp Star of tħe Nigħt (p. 62).—The words of this song are by W. G. T. Moncrieff, and were set to an adaptation of the Copenhagen Waltz, the date of which is 1801. But the air we give was as sung by Mr. Waylett, possibly by Alexander Lee, though Mrs. Waylett is generally credited with having composed it. It was published as hers anyhow.

Mrs. Waylett gave popularity to the song. It was sung by her in 1835. She was a daughter of Cook, an upholsterer in Bath, and born February 7, 1800. She was placed under Loder for her musical education. She married a very wretched actor, Waylett, 17th November 1819, who appeared as Richard III. on the Birmingham stage in 1821. The uproar occasioned by his bad acting rose to such an extent at the end of the third act, that the manager had to appear and entreat the audience to defer judgment till the end of the performance. Immediately after Richard had been killed, the manager stepped before the curtain and said, " Ladies and gentlemen, now you may pronounce your verdict on the departed Richard." Whereupon a stentorian voice from the pit shouted, "Justifiable homicide."

Mrs. Waylett was called the " Queen of Ballad Singers." The story has already been told of her marriage with Alexander Lee, and of her death.

O No, We Never Mention Her (p. 66).—The story of the origin of this song is as follows :—Thomas Haynes Bayly, of whose life an outline has already been given, was at Oxford a student at St. Mary's Hall. He one day received a letter from a young lady at Bath, whom he knew very slightly indeed, entreating him to excuse the liberty she took in addressing him, but pleading in excuse her great anxiety about her brother, a fellow-student of Bayly, who was unwell, and she feared lest he should be suffering from incipient consumption, which had proved fatal to several members of his family. From him she had not received satisfactory accounts, and she had therefore assumed the liberty of writing to Mr. Bayly to entreat him to see her brother and tell her his candid opinion of the young man's case. This led to a correspondence between the poet and the young lady. He visited the invalid, who became very ill, and Bayly watched over him, sat with him, and was with him when he died.

On returning to Bath he was overwhelmed with thanks by the bereaved family for his attention, and invited constantly by the afflicted parents to fill the vacant seat at their table. He did his best to comfort the sorrowing sister, and as " pity is akin to love," it is not surprising that he fell in love with her, and soon proposed. The young lady had nothing of her own, and Haynes Bayly was entirely dependent on his father ; consequently it was not possible for the young couple to be married. They parted never to meet again. The young lady was not so broken-hearted as to refuse an offer from a suitor in better circumstances, and she soon became the wife of another. This preyed upon Bayly's spirits, and for some time he was very melancholy. He was sent, to divert his thoughts, to Scotland, but without much effect at first. It was with thoughts dwelling on his disappointment that he wrote the songs, " O No, we Never Mention her," and " May thy Lot in Life be Happy."

Sir Henry Bishop set the first to music ; the second was set by C. E. Horn.

During the year spent in Scotland Bayly wrote his volume of " Songs to Rosa," in which his feelings at his loss find expression as well. One of these is—

" Yes, we will meet as the coldest have met—
Yes, we will part with no sigh of regret ;
Oh ! if those eyes dare to look upon me,
Why should I shrink from a meeting with thee?

Come with the smile of a saint on thy brow,
Come with the friends who are dear to thee now ;
If in my soul lurks no thought of deceit,
Say, is it I that should blush when we met ?"

J Speaʃk of Tħee (p. 68).—A song by Maria B. Hawes, daughter of William Hawes, for some time director of the music at the English Opera, Lyceum ; and it was under his direction and at his instance that Weber's " Der Freischütz " was first performed in England, July 24, 1824, an event that forms an epoch in the history of the opera in this country. Maria Billington Hawes, afterwards Mrs. Merest, for some time was known as a fine contralto singer ; she was the composer of pleasing ballads.

Awake, Sweet Love (p. 71).—Some account of Dowland has already been given, under the heading of his song, " Now, O Now, we Needs Must Part." The composition " Awake, Sweet Love," is actually a madrigal ; we give it here as a song. Dowland published " The First Booke of Songes or Ayres " in 1595, and the second in 1600. Dr. Crotch included " Awake, Sweet Love," in his collection of specimens of old music.

Cafeħ Quotem (p. 74).—A favourite song from the ballad opera of " The Review, or the Wags of Windsor," by George Colman the younger. It was performed at the Haymarket in 1801. Fawcet enacted the part of the Parish Clerk, and sang the song of " Caleb Quotem," which was composed by William Shield, although the opera was entrusted to Dr. Arnold to set. Fawcet was the son of an actor, but his father was unwilling that his son should take to the boards, and so bound him apprentice to a linen-draper in London. However, he ran away and joined a strolling company. He came out as Caleb in " He would be a Soldier ; " he performed the part of Falstaff, and in " The Review " gained great favour with the song we now give. Miss De Camp sang in the same piece as the " Spruce little Drummer-Boy."

The song has been slightly curtailed by us.

Musidora (p. 80).—A song by Dr. Croft. William Croft was a native of Warwickshire. He was born in 1677, and was trained under Dr. Blow. In 1700 he was admitted Gentleman Extraordinary of the Chapel Royal ; in 1707, upon the decease of Jeremiah Clarke, he was appointed assistant organist to Dr. Blow ; upon whose death, in 1708, he obtained his place. In 1715 he obtained his degree of Doctor of Music, and died in 1727. In the earlier part of his career Croft composed for the theatre, and produced the accidental music for " Courtship à la Mode," 1700 ; " The Funeral," 1702 ; " The Twin Rivals," 1703 ; and " The Dying Loves," 1704. " Musidora " was inserted in the fifth volume of " The Musical Miscellany " of Watts, 1731.

Dear Love, regard mp Grief (p. 84).—The ballad is very ancient. It is " The Noble Lord's Cruelty, or a Pattern of True Love," and occurs in the Roxburghe Collection. It has been reprinted in Mr. Ebsworth's edition, vi. 681-3. Its date is before 1624. The tune to which it was set then was " Daintie, Come Thou to Me." Of this, one version is given by Mr. Chappell in his " Popular Music of the Olden Time," p. 517 of the original edition. It is the tune to which the " Ballad of Whittington " was sung, and goes also by the name of " Whittington's Bells." The ballad of " Daintie, Come Thou to Me," beginning " Wilt thou forsake me thus, and leave me in misery ? " was reprinted in the first volume of the " Roxburghe Ballads," p. 629. Another name for the air was "Ned Smith."

The tune here given is not that of " Daintie, Come Thou to Me," but one taken down at Exbourne from a labouring-man, on the same evening on which "The Torrington Ringers" was noted. The air is very curious and ancient, and seems to date from the Tudor period. In the original ballad there are far too many stanzas to be used.

The Storm (p. 86).—The words by George Alexander Stevens were introduced into a marine medley, and published by him in "The Muses' Delight" in 1754, and again in his "Songs, Comic and Satyrical," in 1772. The song has been somewhat amplified since composed by Incledon. The air that Stevens adopted for it is that of an old sea-song, "Come and Listen to my Ditty," which is found in Walsh's "British Musical Miscellany," 1730. The same is used in the ballad operas of "Robin Hood," 1730, and "Silvia," 1731, where it is called "How Happy are Young Lovers." Glover's ballad of "Hosier's Ghost" was sung to the same air.

Incledon was wont to tell a story relative to the effect that he produced with this song upon Mrs. Siddons :—"She paid me one of the finest compliments I ever received. I sang 'The Storm' after dinner ; she cried and sobbed like a child. Taking both my hands, she said, 'All that I and my brother ever did is nothing to the effect you produce.'" "I remember," says William Robson, in *The Old Playgoer*, "when the *élite* of taste and science and literature were assembled to pay the well-deserved compliment of a dinner to John Kemble, and to present him with a handsome piece of plate on his retirement, Incledon sang, when requested, his best song, ' The Storm.' The effect was sublime, the silence holy, the feeling intense, and while Talma was recovering from his astonishment, Kemble placed his hand on the arm of the great French actor, and said, in an agitated, emphatic, and proud tone, ' *That* is an English singer.' "

"When Rauzzini heard Incledon at Bath rolling his voice grandly up like a surge of the sea, till, touching the top note, it died away in sweetness, he exclaimed in rapture, ' *Corpo di Dio !* it was very lucky there was some roof above, or you would be heard by the angels in heaven and make them jealous.' " (Barker Baker, "The London Stage").

Tell Me Where is Fancy Bred (p. 88.)—The words by Shakespeare, and taken from "The Merchant of Venice." Fancy in Shakespeare and the dramatists and poets of his age is but another word for love. The music by Sir J. Stevenson.

Mrs. Waylett was singing this song at Dublin, when a baker among the "gods," considering this question addressed to him, or that the opportunity for advertisement of his shop was not to be passed by, roared from the gallery—"The best fancy bread is to be had at Lynch's shop in Exchequer Street ; the best in Dublin—devil a better anywhere else."

As written by Sir John Stevenson, the duet was for treble and bass, but was arranged by Bishop for two sopranos, as treble and bass were voices too far apart to make the duet really effective, and Bishop's recast is generally accepted.

The Lass of Baldock Mill (p. 94).—The song was one of those made popular by the singing of Beard, who had his musical education in the Chapel Royal under Bernard Gates. His name first appears in the *dramatis personæ* of Handel's operas, performed at Covent Garden in 1736. He became a great favourite of the town, by his style of singing Galliard's hunting-song, "With Early Horn." His voice was a rich tenor ; he was a thoroughly worthy,

respectable man, and he married the only daughter of the Earl of Waldegrave,* and lived very happily with her for fourteen years till her death. His second wife was the daughter of Rich, then patentee of Covent Garden Theatre, at whose death Beard, in right of his wife, became one of the proprietors of the theatre ; but he sold his share and retired from the stage.

The song "The Lass of Baldock Mill" appears in *The London Magazine* for May 1753, as "sung by Mr. Beard," so also in " Clio and Euterpe," where it is the first song in the second volume, 1759. I have not seen the words attributed to any author.

The melody is the composition of Michael Christopher Festing, one of two sons left orphans by their father, Count Festing, who fell in the battle of Höchstadt, where he was aid-de-camp to Prince Eugene. Marlborough took a fancy to the boys and brought them to England, and they were educated at his charge, and were much about Queen Anne's Court. The orders worn by Count Festing on the field of battle are in the possession of his descendant, Henry Festing, Esq. of Bois Hall, Surrey. Michael Christopher was a pupil of Geminiani, and was a skilful violinist. On the opening of Ranelagh Gardens in 1742, he was appointed director of the music, as well as leader of the band.

To Festing appertains the principal merit of establishing the fund for the support of decayed musicians and their families. This society took its rise in the year 1738 from the following occurrence :—Festing, being one day seated at the window of the Orange coffee-house, at the corner of the Haymarket, noticed an intelligent-looking boy driving an ass and selling brick-dust. He was in rags. Something induced Festing to descend and speak to him, when he learned that he was the son of an unfortunate musician. Struck with pity at the thought that this poor lad in distressing poverty should be the child of a brother professional, Festing determined to attempt something for the child's support. He consulted Dr. Maurice Green, whose son had married his daughter, and these worthy men together established a fund for the support of decayed musicians and their families.

Michael Christopher Festing's brother John was an oboist and teacher of the flute, and died in 1772. Michael Christopher died in 1752.

The Gallant Sailor (p. 96).—This song can be traced back to about 1770, when it appears in half-sheet with music ; it also occurs in several collections of songs. It is found in Calliope, 1788. The war referred to is that of 1756-9, when the French made preparations to invade England. As in the original there are but four lines, and each piece is sung twice, I have added two to each verse.

Torrington Ringers (p. 101).—One example out of an entire class of songs belonging to Bell-ringing. I have taken down a great many of them, of various qualities. One, especially good, was given in " Songs of the West." That now inserted in "English Minstrelsie" was procured from an old ringer at Exbourne, near Hatherleigh. Mr. Bussell had invited some singers to meet me one evening, and this was one of the songs produced. I wrote to the Rector of Black Torrington relative to the names introduced into the song, and his answer was: " Yesterday I had my yearly dinner to the old people of the parish, when we had a long talk relative to the song you sent me. About fifty years ago there was a blacksmith, a ringer ; his name was John Wait. The doctor in 1877 was called Tapley. I can find no record of the names of Turner or Sweet in the registers." With regard to another song of

---

* Harriet, only daughter of James, first Earl of Waldegrave, was married first to Lord Edward Herbert ; it was as a widow that she ran away with Beard.

Bell-ringing relative to Egloshayle in Cornwall, I was able to discover and fix the date of all the ringers named; but in this instance the air of the song was several centuries earlier than their date. It was, in fact, an archaic tune of Henry VII.'s reign.

𝕾𝖜𝖊𝖊𝖙 𝖆𝖗𝖊 𝖙𝖍𝖊 𝕮𝖍𝖆𝖗𝖒𝖘 𝖔𝖋 𝕳𝖊𝖗 𝕴 𝕷𝖔𝖛𝖊 (p. 104).—
The air is employed in "The Fashionable Lady," 1730, as a dialogue between four voices, "Spare, O Spare the Hum'rous Sage." The same air occurs in "The Village Opera," 1729, for a song, "Oh! Tell us, Cupid, Heav'nly Boy." The original words are found in "The Hive," 1724, vol. i. p. 122, in seven stanzas, and were the composition of Barton Booth. Ritson prints them in his "Collection of English Songs."

Barton Booth, born in 1681, was the youngest son of a Lancashire squire. He was educated at Westminster School, but took to the stage, and made his first appearance in Smock Alley Theatre, Dublin, 1698. His first appearance in London was in 1700. In 1704 he married the daughter of Sir William Barkham, Bart., of Norfolk; she died in 1710, and nine years later he married Hester Santlow, the dancer, to whom he was passionately attached, and in whose virtue he was a firm believer, although scandal declared that she had lived under the protection of the Duke of Marlborough, and after that, of Secretary Craggs. Booth died in 1733. He was the author of "The Death of Dido," a masque, 1716, and some poems of no extraordinary merit, but not without grace.

The air was composed by Leveridge.

𝕭𝖗𝖚𝖙𝖚𝖘 (p. 106).—A cantata, the words by W. Smith, of St. Peter's College, Cambridge, and the music by William Beale.

Beale was a Cornishman, born at Landrake on New Year's Day, 1784, and was brought up as a chorister of Westminster Abbey, under Dr. Arnold and Robert Cooke. In 1813 he gained the prize cup given by the Madrigal Society, having won it by his madrigal "Awake, sweet Muse." In 1820 he published a collection of his glees and madrigals. Among his songs none was so favoured by amateurs as "Brutus." Beale died in London in 1854.

𝕳𝖆𝖗𝖊𝖘 𝖎𝖓 𝖙𝖍𝖊 𝕺𝖑𝖉 𝕻𝖑𝖆𝖓𝖙𝖆𝖙𝖎𝖔𝖓 (p. 110).—A folk-song, one of the favourite series of poaching ditties. It comes from Yorkshire, and was published by Mr. F. Kidson in his "Traditional Tunes." We have ventured to add a slight chorus, to impart some briskness to the song, and to slightly vary the notes to "away in the old plantation;" as Mr. Kidson gives it, it is f, a, bb, c. There are a good many verses in the original of no great value. I have added a conclusion, which is lacking in the song as taken down.

𝕮𝖊𝖆𝖘𝖊 𝖞𝖔𝖚𝖗 𝕱𝖚𝖓𝖓𝖎𝖓𝖌 (p. 112).—This is a song, the music of which is supposed to have been composed for "The Beggars' Opera," but, if so, by whom is utterly unknown. It is, however, possible that it was an old tune that Gay used, without knowing what were the words that had originally been sung to it. There are half-sheet songs to the same tune, such as "Charming Billy," that commences "When the hills and lofty mountains;" but we cannot say that these are earlier than "The Beggars' Opera."

John Parry, in 1833, touched up the air, as he touched up "The Women all tell me I'm False to my Lass," and set to it Welsh words, "Llwyn-on," or "The Ash Grove." It had already appeared in the "Bardic Museum" of Edward Jones, 1802, who called it after the name of his own house, Llwynn-onn, near Wrexham. Jones' version is a reminiscence, but one not very accurate, of "Cease your Funning," and is probably due to Mr. Jones himself, as it is not contained in earlier collections of Welsh music. From "The

Beggars' Opera" the air was imported into "The Fashionable Lady," 1730, where to it is set the 30th song:—

> "Idle creature!
> Form and feature
> Give thy anxious soul its pain;
> Pretty faces,
> Modish graces,
> O'er thy conquered reason reign."

The song, "Cease your Funning," has, in the play, but one stanza, I have added a second.

𝕺! 𝕸𝖔𝖙𝖍𝖊𝖗, 𝖆 𝕳𝖔𝖔𝖕 (p. 114).—There are two versions of this old English song—one as a solo, the other as a duet. The latter is entitled "A Dialogue between Miss Molly and her Mother about a Hoop." It consists of ten stanzas, of which Mr. Chappell has extracted four for his "Popular Music of the Olden Time."

In some broadsides with the music the air is attributed to one Brailsford, who composed songs about 1728, at which date he contributed one to Cibber's play of "Love in a Riddle." On an early engraved half-sheet music, however, the air is attributed to Nicolas Nemo, a London organist.

Hoops came into fashion about 1711, which is the date of the song. The air became popular, and Cibber wrote to it the song of "What Woman could Do, I have Tried, to be Free," for his ballad opera of "Love in a Riddle," 1729. In "The Livery Rake," 1733 it has a song set to it beginning, "When woman once gets a man in her head." Another song is set to it in "Damon and Phillida," 1734.

The original words concern the fashion of wearing hoops; the daughter urges her mother to get her one, and to this the mother raises objections. The best verse is this:—

> "Pray hear me, dear mother, what I have been taught,
> Nine men and nine women o'erset in a boat;
> The men were all drown'd, but the women did float,
> And by the help of their hoops they all safely got out."

I have thought it advisable to rewrite the song in three stanzas.

𝕿𝖍𝖊 𝕸𝖎𝖑𝖑𝖊𝖗'𝖘 𝖂𝖊𝖉𝖉𝖎𝖓𝖌 (p. 116).—In 1751 the successful pantomime of "Harlequin Ranger" was produced at Drury Lane. The words were by Henry Woodward. Woodward was a tallow-chandler's son in Southwark, and he was born in 1717, and educated at Merchant Taylors' School. His father intended him to continue in the business, but an accident diverted the current of his life. On account of the extraordinary run of the "Beggars' Opera," Rich, the manager of the Theatre Royal in Lincoln's Inn Fields, was encouraged to represent it by children. Into this Lilliputian company young Woodward, at the age of fourteen, was drawn, and he performed the part of Peachum with great success, and was so caught with the stage fever that he got himself bound apprentice to Rich. He played at first inferior characters, till he arrived at that of Harlequin, which was the summit of his ambition. However, he did not remain stationary when he had attained the spangles and motley and bat of Harlequin, but proceeded to act in parts that required some ability, and he did this with considerable applause. In 1747 Mr. Sheridan, manager of Smock Alley Theatre, Dublin, engaged him at a salary of £500 to perform the ensuing winter. In this engagement Woodward was articled as a comedian and harlequin. On his return to England he was at once engaged by Garrick for Drury Lane. After some years Woodward had saved over £6000, and then he was ambitious to become a manager. For this purpose he joined with Barry, who was at this time at Covent Garden, in an attempt to oppose Sheridan in Dublin. For this purpose a new house was erected by them in Crow Street, and on the 22nd October 1753 they opened it with the comedy of "She Would, and She Would Not," to a very thin audience. The second night was the "Beggars' Opera," and the take was but £20.

The managers now quarrelled, and Woodward withdrew his share, on getting security to be paid his original outlay in yearly instalments.

During his residence in Dublin a ludicrous circumstance happened. He lodged immediately opposite the Parliament House, in College Green. One day a riot broke out, and the Parliament House was beset by the rabble in order to prevent the passing of an unpopular Bill. The ringleaders arrested the representatives, and resolved to make them swear to oppose the measure. They made a rush for Woodward's house, and shouted to him to throw them down a Bible. As it happened, there was none in the house, but Woodward picked up a Shakespeare and cast it down to the crowd, and the ignorant rioters at once proceeded to swear the members on this volume.

London about 1696, and received his musical education as a chorister of St. Paul's Cathedral. In 1716 he obtained the appointment of organist of St. Dunstan's-in-the-West, Fleet Street, and on the death of Daniel Purcell, in 1717, was chosen organist of St. Andrew's, Holborn. In 1718 he became organist of St. Paul's Cathedral, and in 1727, on the death of Dr. Croft, organist and composer to the Chapel-Royal. He succeeded the excellent John Eccles in 1735 as Master of the King's Band. He died in 1755, leaving an only daughter, married to the Rev. Michael Festing, son of the German violinist, who had for some time conducted the Vauxhall concerts. A portrait of Dr. Green, by an unknown artist, is in the possession of his descendant, Henry Festing, Esq. of Bois Hall, Addleston. By

DOCTOR MAURICE GREEN.

Woodward died in 1777, and left the interest of his fortune, which amounted to £6000, to Miss Bellamy, the actress, with whom he had lived in close friendship for some time before his death.

The song of "Ralph of the Mill," which occurs in "Harlequin Ranger," became very popular. The air was probably already familiar, and the words were pleasant. The name of the composer is not given. It is found in "Apollo's Cabinet," 1757; in "Clio and Euterpe," 1758; and in the *London Magazine* for February 1752, and is found in half-sheet engraved songs.

Fair Sally Loved a Gallant Seaman (p. 118).—
Doctor Maurice Green, the composer of this song, was born in

his kind permission we are enabled to give an engraving of this beautiful picture. A second portrait by Hayman is possessed by C. T. Johnson, Esq., 1 Alwyne Place, Canonbury.

The song "Fair Sally Loved a Gallant Seaman" is attributed in some books to Mr. Percy. This is not Bishop Percy, who was born in 1728, but John Percy, of whom something shall be said later on. Percy published the song with his own air to it, but this did not take; and Green wrote to it the delightful melody we give, and which at once "caught on" with the public. The song appears in "Calliope," vol. i., in 1739, and in "The Universal Harmony," 1745; in "Apollo's Banquet," 1757; and it appears on half-sheets of about 1740.

INDEX TO SONGS--VOL. IV.

• In cases where the First Line differs from the Title, the former is also given (in italics). The figures in parentheses refer to the page at which the NOTE will be found.

Tell me, Mary, how to woo Thee.

G. A. HODSON.
(W. H. H.)

Tell me, Ma-ry, how to woo thee, Teach my bo-som to re-veal.....

ritard.

All its sor-rows sweet un-to thee, All the love my heart can feel;

colla voce

Tell me, Ma-ry how to woo thee, Teach my bo-som to re-veal

_p_

All its sorrows sweet un-to thee, All the love my heart can feel.

_f_

No! when joy first bright-en'd o'er us,

_p_

'Twas not joy il-lum'd her ray, And when sor-row lies be-fore us,

'Twill not chase her smiles a-way, 'Twill not chase her smiles a-way,

'Twill not chase her smiles a-way. Tell me, Ma-ry, how to woo thee,

Teach my bo-som to re-veal All its sor-rows sweet un-to thee,

All the love my heart can feel.

Key C. Like the tree no winds can se - ver From the i - vy round it cast,

Thus the heart that lov'd thee ev - er, Loves thee, Ma - ry, Loves thee, Ma - ry,

Loves thee, Ma - ry, to the last. Tell me, Ma - ry, how to woo thee,

Teach my bo-som to re-veal All its sor-rows sweet un-to thee,

All the love my heart can feel, All its sor-rows sweet un-to thee,

All its sor-rows sweet un-to thee, All the love my heart can feel,

All the love my heart can feel, All the love my heart can feel.

THE PILGRIM OF LOVE.

Words by DIMOND.

Sir H. R. BISHOP.
(W. H. H.)

O - ryn - thia, my be - lov - ed!   I call in vain!

Andante.

p dolce

Key B♭.

A Her - mit who dwells in these so - li - tudes cross'd me, As way - worn and faint up the
"Yet tar - ry, my son, till the burning noon pass - es, Let boughs of the lemon tree

pp stacc.

moun-tain I press'd, The a - ged man paus'd on his staff to ac - cost me, And
shel - ter thy head, The juice of ripe Mus - ca - del flows in my glass - es, And

Now, O now I needs must part.

JOHN DOWLAND. 1627
(H. F. S.)

Key C.

turn.
hour.

|d :— :— | : : |d' :— :d' |d' :— :m' |r' :— :m' |r' :— :—

While I live I needs must love,
Nev - er - more for me shall rise

Key G.

|d' :d' :t |l :d' :t | l :— :— | —:— :— |m :— :r |d :— :t,

Love lives not when life is done,
Gold - en glad the morn - ing sun,

Now at last de -
Ev - er - more, in

rall.   *a tempo*   *cres.*

rall.   ad lib.

|l, :— :d |r :— :⌣ | m :s :f |—.f :m :r | d :— :— | —:— :— | : :| : :||

spair does prove   Love di - vi - ded lov - eth none.
dark - 'ning eyes   Set - ting life and light are done.

f rall.   *dim.*

3.

Sad despair doth drive me hence,
That despair unkindness sends,
If that parting be offence,
It is she which then offends,

4.

And although your sight I leave,
Sight where'er my joys do lie,
Till that death do sense bereave
Never shall affection die.

THE DEEP, DEEP SEA.

Words by Mrs GEORGE SHARPE.

C. HORN. (W. H. H.)

Oh, come with me, my love, And our fai - ry home shall be, Where the

water spi - rits rove, In the deep, deep sea, In the

deep, deep sea, In the deep, deep sea.

Key G.

There are jew - els rich and rare, In the ca - verns of the deep, And to

braid thy ra - ven hair There the pear - ly trea - sures sleep; In a

ti - ny man of war, Thou shalt stem the o - cean's tide, Or

Key C.

in a cry - stal sea, Sit a queen in all her pride, Oh,____

come with me, my love, And our fai - ry home shall be In the deep, deep

sea, In the deep, deep sea.

Ah, be-lieve that love may dwell Where the

co-ral branch-es twine, And that ev-'ry wreathed shell, Breathes a

tone as soft as thine. Hopes as fond, as thou would'st prove,

se :–:l |t :–:m | l :–:t |d' :–: | d' :–:f |f :–:f | f :–:m |m :–:m
Truth as bright as e'er was told, Hearts as warm as those a- bove, Dwell

|l :r :r |re :–:re | m:–:–:–: | f :–:|m :–:r | m :–:m:–:–| l :–:–:l̂ :–: s
un-der the wa - ters cold, Un- der the wa - ters cold___ Oh,

|d' :t :d' |r' :–:t | d' :–: | s :d' | t :–:|l | s :–:f | m :–:|d':t :d' | s :–:|l :–:
come with me, my love, And our fai - ry home shall be In the deep, deep

|r :–:|m:r :m | d :–:–:r :m | d :–:–:–: | d' :–:ta |s :–:m | f :–:–| :m :f
sea, In the deep, deep sea,___ Come with me, my love, And our

TUBAL CAIN.

Words by C. MACKAY.

Music by H. RUSSELL.
(W. H. H.)

lord.

true.

3.

But a sudden change came o'er his head,
　Ere the setting of the sun,
And Tubal Cain was filled with pain,
　For the evil he had done;
He saw that men with rage and hate
　Made war upon their kind,
And the land was red with the blood they shed
　In their lust for carnage blind
And he said, alas! that e'er I made,
　Or skill of mine should plan
The spear and sword for men who joy
　To slay their fellow-man.

4.

And for many a day old Tubal Cain
　Sat brooding o'er his woe;
His hand forbore to smite the ore,
　His furnace smoulder'd low;
At last he rose with cheerful face
　And bright courageous eye,
And bared his strong right arm for work
　While the quick flame mounted high.
And he sang, Hurra! for my handiwork,
　And the red sparks lit the air;
Not alone for the blade was the bright steel made,
　And he fashioned the first ploughshare.

5.

And men, taught wisdom from the past,
　In friendship joined their hands,
Hung sword in hall and spear on wall,
　And they ploughed the willing land,
They sang, Hurra! for Tubal Cain,
　Our staunch good friend is he,
And for the ploughshare and the plough
　To him our praise shall be.
But while oppression lifts its head
　Or tyrant would be lord,
Though we may thank him for the plough,
　We'll not forget the sword

Quaff with Me the Purple Wine.

SHIELD. (W. H. H.)

me the beau - teous fair, And dance off hea - vy, hea - vy care, And

dance off hea - vy, hea - vy care, And dance off hea - vy, hea - - -

- vy, hea - - - - - vy care, And dance off hea - - vy

care.

Key F.
Lah is D.

Wine in -

24

THE GIRL I LEFT BEHIND ME.

Smoothly and briskly.

Music, English March
of the 18th cent. (W. H. H.)

Key Eb.

I'm lonesome since I cross'd the hill, And o'er the moor and val - ley, Such
Oh, ne'er shall I for - get the night, The stars were bright a - bove me, And

hea - vy thoughts my heart do fill Since part - ing with my Sal - ly; I
gent - ly lent their silv' - ry light, When first she vow'd to love me! But

seek no more the fine or gay, For each does but re - mind me, How
now I'm bound to Brigh - ton camp, Kind Hea - ven then pray guide me, And

swift- ly pass'd the hours a - way With the girl I left be - hind me.
send me safe - ly back a - gain To the girl I left be - hind me.

3

Her golden hair in ringlets fair,
 Her eyes like diamonds shining,
Her slender waist, her carriage chaste,
 May leave the swan repining.
Ye gods above! oh, hear my prayer.
 To my beauteous fair to bind me,
And send me safely back again
 To the girl I left behind me.

4

The bee shall honey taste no more,
 The dove become a ranger,
The falling waters cease to roar,
 Ere I shall seek to change her.
The vows we register'd above
 Shall ever cheer and bind me
In constancy to her I love,
 To the girl I left behind me.

HEART OF OAK.

Words by D. GARRICK.

Dr. BOYCE. (W. H. H.)

Key A.

```
{: s₁ | d :d ,d | d :m ,r | d :t₁ ,l₁ |s₁ : .s₁}
   Come, cheer up, my lads,'tis to glo-ry we steer,   To
   We ne'er see our foes but we wish them to stay,   They
```

```
{| l₁ :l₁ ,t₁ | d :d ,r | m :f ,r | m :s₁ .s₁ | d :m₁ ,f₁ |s₁ :l₁ ,t₁ |
   add something more to this won-der-ful year,   To hon-our we call you, not
   nev-er see us but they wish us a-way;   If they run, why we fol-low, and
```

press you like slaves, For who are so free as the sons of the waves?
run them a - shore, For if they wont fight us we can - not do more. Heart of

oak are our ships, Heart of oak are our men, We al - ways are rea-dy,

stea - dy, boys, stea - dy, We'll fight and we'll con-quer a - gain and a - gain.

Still Briton shall triumph, her ships plough the sea,
Her standard be Justice, her watch word "Be free;
Then cheer up my lads, with one heart let us sing,
Our Soldiers, our Sailors, our Statesmen, our King.
Heart of Oak &c.

Words by JAMES COBB.

STORACE. (W. H. H.)

Slowly and with expression.

Piano.

Key Ab.

With low-ly suit and plain-tive dit-ty I call the

ten - der mind to pi-ty, I call the

ten - der mind to pi-ty; My friends are gone, my heart is

beat - ing, And chill - ing pov - er - ty's my lot. From pass-ing stran - gers aid en-

treat-ing, I wan - der thus a - lone, for - got. Re-lieve my woes, my wants dis-

tress-ing, And heav'n re - ward you with its bless-ing.

cres.   *dim.*

Here tales of love and maids for - sak-en; Of bat - tles fought and cap - tives

tak-en;   The jo - vial tar   so bold-ly   sail - ing,   Or cast up - on some de - sert

shore,   The hap - less bride   his loss be - wail-ing,___   And fear- ing ne'er   to see him

more.   Re-lieve my   woes,   my wants   dis - tress-ing,   And heav'n re -

ward you   with   its   bless-ing.

CELEBRATE THIS FESTIVAL.

H. PURCELL.
(H. F. S.)

E. 4. c.

Gracefully.

Kind - ly treat Ma - ri - a's day, And your hom - age 'twill ___ re - pay, - pay, Be - queath - ing bless - ings on our isle The te - dious mo - ments to ___ be guile, Till conquest, till conquest, till con - quest to Ma - ri - a's

THE ROSE THAT WEEPS.

W. HORSLEY
(W. H. H.)

The rose that weeps with mor - ning dew, And
The dews that bend the blush - ing flow'r En-

glit-ters in the sun - ny ray, In tears and smiles re-
-rich the scent, re - new the glow, So love's sweet tears ex-

In this old chair my Father sat.

Words by EDWARD FITZBALL.

M. W. BALFE. (W. H. H.)

Key B♭.

In this old chair my fa - ther sat, In this my
And here, a - las! when they were gone, In beau - ty's

mo - ther smil'd; I hear their bles - sings on me wait, And feel my -
own ar - ray, A pity - ing an - gel on me shone To chase each

self a child; I feel the kiss of their fond love, Oh, joy! oh,
grief a - way; But oh! it was de - lu - sive love, A - las! too

joy too bright to last! Ah! why will cru - el time re -
sweet, too pure to last! And if such dream time must re -

move, Or mem'- ry paint the past, Or mem'- ry paint the
move, Why mem'- ry paint the past, Why mem'- ry paint the

past?
past?

MEET ME BY MOONLIGHT ALONE.

J. A. WADE. (W. H. H.)

said, / there,   I would show the night flow-ers their queen; — Nay, turn not a-
For tho' dear-ly a moon-light I prize, — I care not for

way that sweet head, — 'Tis the love-li - est e - ver was seen! — } Oh!
all in the air — If I want the sweet light of your eyes. —

meet me by moon-light a - lone, — Meet me by moon-light a - lone. —

Through the Wood.

Words by
W. H. BELLAMY.

Music by
C. E. HORN. (H. F. S.)

Thro' the wood, thro' the wood, fol - low and find me, Search ev' - ry hol - low and

din - gle and dell;— I leave not the print of a foot-step be - hind me, So

they that would see me must seek for me well.

Key B♭.

Look in the li - ly - bell, ruf - fle the rose, Un - der the leaves of the

vi - o - let peep, Lull'd by a ze-phyr in cra-dles like those

Key E♭.

All the day long you may catch me a-sleep, Thro' the wood, thro' the wood,

fol - low and find me, Search ev'-ry hol-low and din-gle and dell; I

leave not the print of a foot-step be-hind me, So they that would see me must

look for me well.

Lah is C.

When the red sun sets at

eve, you may hear me Sing-ing fare-well to his rays as they fade, But as

soon as the step of a mor-tal is near me I take to my wings and fly off to the shade.

ad lib.   *ritard.*

ad lib.

Key E♭.

Thro' the wood, thro' the wood, seek till you find me; Haste, for at night-fall the

blos-soms will close, Fol-low, fol-low, fol-low and find me;

fol-low, fol-low, fol-low and find me.

Tom Bowling.

Andante con espressione.

C. DIBDIN (W. H. H.)

3

Yet shall poor Tom find pleasant weather,
When He who all commands
Shall give, to call life's crew together,
The word to pipe all hands.
Thus Death, who kings and tars despatches,
In vain Tom's life has doff'd;
For though his body's under hatches,
His soul has gone aloft.

THE ROAST BEEF OF OLD ENGLAND.

LEVERIDGE (W. H. H.)

When might-y roast beef was the Eng-lish-man's food, It en - no - bled our hearts and en -
But since we have learn'd from ef - fem- i - nate France To eat their ra - gouts as

rich - ed our blood; Our sol -diers were brave and our cour - tiers were good.
well as to dance, We are fed up with no-thing but vain com - plai - sance.

Oh, the roast beef Of old Eng - land! and oh! for Old Eng - lands roast beef.

3

Our fathers of old were robust, stout and strong,
And kept open house, with good cheer all day long,
Which made their plump tenants rejoice in the song.
    Oh! the, &c.

4

When good Queen Elizabeth sat on the throne,
Ere coffee and tea, and such slip-slops were known,
The world was in terror if e'en she should frown.
    Oh! the, &c.

5

In those days if fleets did presume on the main,
They seldom or never returned back again;
As witness the vaunting Armada of Spain.
    Oh! the, &c.

6

Oh, then we had stomachs to eat and to fight,
And when wrong were cooking. to set ourselves right;
But now we're a-hm!-- I could, but good night.
    Oh! the, &c.

FLY! FLY! YE LAZY HOURS.

JOHN ECCLES.
(H. F. S.)

Fly! fly! ye la - zy hours, Bring here my love,
Fie! fie! thou slug - gish time, Why this de - lay?

Swift be your flight, Swift be your flight as my Fond wish - es move.
Let thoughts of youth, Let thoughts of youth and love Urge thy slow way.

Fly! fly! ye la - zy hours, Bring here my love,
Fie! fie! thou slug - gish time, Why this de - lay?

Swift be your flight, Swift be your flight as my Fond wish-es move; When we
Let thoughts of youth, Let thoughts of youth and love Urge thy slow way, With the

love, and love to rage, Ev-'ry mo-ment seems an age, When we
mem'-ry of her charms, Speed my lov-er to these arms With the

love, and love to rage, Ev-'ry mo-ment seems an age.
mem-'ry of her charms, Speed my lov-er to these arms.

OLD ADAM.

Folk Air.
(H. F. S.)

Key D.
Old   A - dam was a poach - er, Went   out one day at fall,   To——
A   keep - er that was pass - ing Peep'd sly - ly thro' the brake, Saw——

```
{ l₁ .d :m .s | m    :d .t₁ | l₁ .d :t₁ .d | l₁    :— ||
catch a hare for roast - ing And  eat - ing, bones and all;
A - dam and his sprin - gle, Pro - ceed - ed both to take.
```

rall.

Major.

```
{ r .l :d' .l | f  .l :d' .l | f .s :l .t | d'   :— .l
In the sun  ex - pect - ing fun Old   A - dam smil - ing lay,  O
Hare wasn't his'n, so in pri - son Old A - dam groan - ing lay, O
```

a tempo

```
{ s .s :s .l | s    :m .r | d .m :r .m | d    :— ||
hare, it is best eat - ing, This  did old A - dam say.
hare, it is good eat - ing, But  not for him to - day.
```

p

WHEN DAISIES PIED.

SHAKESPEARE.

In pastoral style.

Dr ARNE. (H. F. S)

Piano.

Key F. When daisies pied and
When shepherds pipe on

vi-o-lets blue, And la - dy-smocks all sil - ver white, And cuckoo buds of yel-low hue Do
oat - en straws, And mer - ry larks are ploughmen's clocks, When turtles tread and rooks and daws, And

paint the mea-dows with delight,
maid - ens bleach their sum-mer smocks,

The Cuckoo then on

ev - 'ry tree Mocks married men, mocks married men, mocks married men, For thus sings he,

Cuc-koo, Cuc-koo, Cuc-koo, Cuc-koo, Cuc-koo,

8ve lower, ad lib.

O word of fear! O word of fear! Un - pleas - ing to a

f

mar - ried ear, Un - pleasing to a mar - ried ear.

rall.

LOVE LIES A BLEEDING.

Old English Air. (H. F. S.)

Piano.

Key F.
Lah is D.

| l₁ ,t₁ :d ,r | m :l₁ | l :se ,l |

La - dy, un - heed-ing, Love lies a-
Love I do nour-ish Yet I not

| t :m | d¹ :t ,l₁ | s ,f :m | r ,m :d ,r | t₁ :s₁ | d :l₁ ,l₁ | d :s₁ |

bleed-ing, Life as a cap - tive Sad - ly I'm lead - ing, Much I ad - mire;
flour-ish, See - ing you others love I grow most cur - rish, Yourchains have bound me,

| d :l₁ ,l₁ | r :t₁ | s ,l :s ,f | m ,r :d | r ,m :d ,r | t₁ :l₁ |

Though I a - spire, Thy heart an ic - i - cle, Mine is all fire.
Your glan-ces woundme, And all your plea-sure is But to con - found me.

Oh, No! My Love, No!

Words by M. G. LEWIS.

M. KELLY (W. H. H.)

own it would please me at home could you tar-ry, Nor e'er feel a wish from Ma-
lieve you too kind for one mo-ment to grieve me, Or to plant in a heart that a-

ri - a to go, But if it gives plea-sure to you, my dear Har-ry, Shall I
dores you such woe; Yet should you dis - hon-our my truth and de - ceive me, Should I

blame your de - par-ture? Oh, no! my love, no! Shall I blame your de-
e'er cease to love you? Oh, no! my love, no! Should I e'er cease to

par-ture? Oh, no! my love, no!
love you? Oh, no! my love, no!

PRETTY STAR OF THE NIGHT.

Words by W. G. T. MONCRIEFF.

Composer Unknown. (H. F. S.)

Key Eb. {.d.r | m :m :m |m :r :m | f :s :l |s .m :-:d.r}

The day star has long been sunk un-der the bil-low, And

mourn-ing in sighs; Then quick-ly, my dear-est, a - rise from your pil-low, And

make the night day with the light of your eyes, And make the night day with the

ad lib.

light of your eyes.

colla voce

rall.

2

Pretty star of my soul, other stars all outshining,
Sweet dream of my slumbers, ah love! pray you, rise:
Enchantress, all hearts in your fetters entwining,
To my ears you are music, and light to mine eyes;
To my anguish you're balm, to my pleasures you're bliss;
To my touch you are joy, there's the world in your kiss;
Day is not day to me if your presence I miss,
Ah no! 'tis a night cold and moonless as this!
        Pretty star of my soul, &c.

Oh No, We Never Mention Her!

Words by T. H. BAYLEY.

Sir H. R. BISHOP. (W. H. H.)

Key G. { .s₁ | d   .,t₁ :d .,r.— | m   .,m :s .m | r   .,d :r .,m.— | d | .s₁ }

Oh no,   we nev-er   men - tion her! Her   name   is nev-er   heard;   My
They bid   me seek in   change of scene, The   charms that o - thers   see,   But

{ d   .,t₁ :d   .,r | m   .,m :s .m | r   .,d :r .m | d | .s }

lips   are now   for - bid   to speak That   once   fa - mil - iar   word.   From
were   I in   a   fo - reignland,They'd   find   no change in   me.   'Tis

sport to sport they hur-ry me, To ban-ish my re-gret, And
true that I be hold no more, The val-ley where we met, I

when they win a smile from me, They think that I for - get.
do not see the haw - thorntree, But how can I for - get.

3

For oh! there are so many things
  Recall the past to me:
The breeze upon the sunny hills,
  The billows of the sea,
The rosy tint that decks the sky
  Before the sun is set,
Ay, ev'ry leaf I look upon,
  Forbids me to forget.

4

They tell me she is happy now
  The gayest of the gay;
They hint that she forgeteth me;
  But I heed not what they say;
Like me, perhaps, she struggles with
  Each feeling of regret,
But if she loves as I have lov'd,
  She never can forget.

I'LL SPEAK OF THEE.

M. M. G. DOWLING.

MARIA B. HAWES.
(H. F. S.)

Pure as yon sky's ce-les-tial blue   My love shall be, my love shall be.

1st Verse.   2nd Verse.

2

Through youth's gay scene, in riper age,
In later life's concluding stage,
Dying, shall thoughts of thee engage
My memory, my memory.
Remember then, remember me,
Remember all I've said to thee;
And my responsive pledge shall be
"I'll speak of thee, I'll speak of thee."
I'll speak of thee, I'll love thee, too,
Fondly and with affection true;
Pure as yon sky's celestial blue
My love shall be, my love shall be.

Awake, sweet Love.

From 'Ayres of foure parts!'
JNO. DOWLAND. 1597 (?)
(H. F. S.)

With tenderness.

For a Second Voice ad lib. or Cello accompaniment ad lib.

Voice.

Piano.

Key F.

A - wake, sweet love, thou art re - turn'd; My heart which

A - wake, sweet love, thou art re - turn'd;

My heart which long in ab - sence mourn'd Lives now in per - fect joy.

long in ab - sence mourn'd Lives now in per - fect joy.

CALEB QUOTEM.

Allegretto.

SHIELD. (W. H. H.)

Voice.

Piano. *mf*

Key C. | s | s .m¹ :r¹ .d¹ | t .l :s .f {

I'm par - ish clerk and sex - ton here, My

{ m .f :s .m | f .r :s | s .m¹:r¹.d¹ | t .l :s .f | m .s :l .r¹ }

name is Cal - eb Quo-tem. I'm pain-ter, gla-zier, auc-tion-eer, In short, I am fac-

to - tum. I make a watch, I mend a pump, For plumber's work my knack is; I

phy - sic sell, I clip the hairs, I tomb-stones cut, I box the ears of lit - tle school-boy

Jackies, of lit - tle school- boy Jackies, I'm par-ish clerk and sex - ton here, My

name is Cal - eb Quo - tem. I'm pain - ter, gla - zier, auc - tion - eer, In

short, I am fac - to - tum!

Ge - o - graph - y is my de - light, Bal-lads and ep - i - taphs I write,

Al - ma - nacks I can in - dite, And graves I dig com - pact and tight.

rall.

colla voce

Vivace.

Key G. At dusk by the fire, like a jol - ly old cock, When my busi-ness is done and all

o-ver, I tip-ple and smoke, by a fire of old oak, By sweet Mis-tress Quo-tem, in

clo-ver, By sweet Mis-tress Quo-tem in clo-ver. With my A - men, A - men,

sing ye lay-men, Bells a ring-ing, Psalms a sing-ing, Graves a dig-ging,

Heads a wig-ging, Keep-ing things go-ing all o-ver the shop. Glaz-ing, braz-ing,

goods ap-prais-ing, Sign-boards writ-ing, Bills in-dit-ing, Trade ad-vis-ing,

Ad - ver - tis - ing, Man - u - fact -'ring lem - o - nade and gin - ger pop Then it's

who'll give a bid for this fine bit of crock-er - y, This e-le-gant wind-up clock-er-y, This

hand-some piece of frock-er - y? What are you go-ing to say for this box of toi-let soap?

cres.

Here you are, come give a bid, they're go - ing! go - ing! go - ing! I

dab-ble in al - most ev' - ry - thing, And keep up lots of fun. And it's

heigh-ho, for Cal - eb Quo - tem, ho! And it's heigh- ho, for Cal - eb Quo - tem ho! Cal - eb

Quo-tem ho! Cal - eb Quo - tem!

MUSIDORA.

Dr. W. CROFT, 1717.
(H. F. S.)

tak - ing   my   dear for the   god - dess Au - ro - ra.

Jes - samines and ros-es A thou - sand pret-ty

pos-ies, The sum - mer's Queen dis-clos- es and strews as she walks.

rall.

A thou - sand pret-ty pos - ies The sum - mer's Queen dis-

tempo

E. 4. f.

clos - es, and strews as she walks. O Ve - nus! O how sweet are the

cool - ing breeze, and the bloom - ing trees, When in - to his bow - er Love

guides Mu - si - do - ra.

Pas - sion, de - vo - tion she gains with each mo - tion; Lutes, too, and

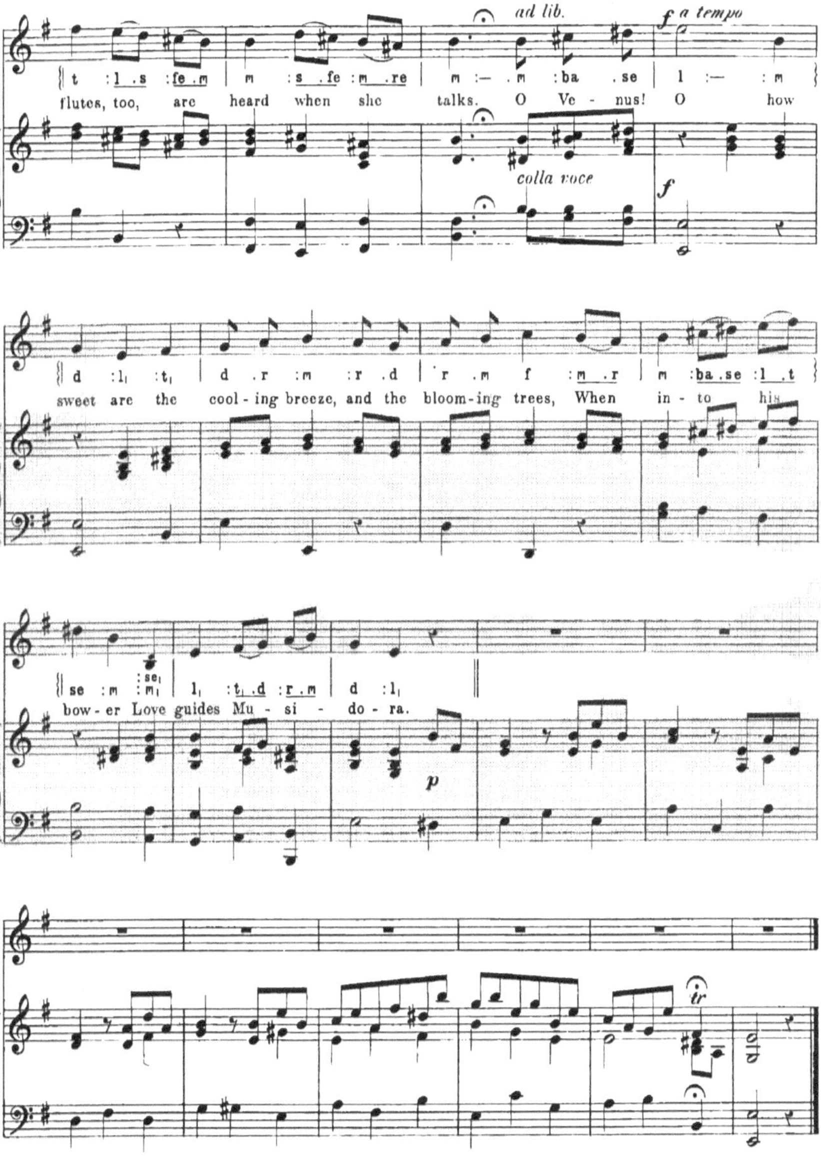
ad lib.
f a tempo
t :l .s :fe .m | m :s .fe :m .re | m :— .m :ba .se | l :— :m
flutes, too, are heard when she talks. O Ve - nus! O how
colla voce
f
d :l, :t, | d .r :m :r .d | r .m f :m .r | m :ba .se :l .t
sweet are the cool - ing breeze, and the bloom - ing trees, When in - to his
se :m :se, m, | l, :t, .d :r .m | d :l,
bow - er Love guides Mu - si - do - ra.
p
tr

DEAR LOVE, REGARD MY GRIEF.

Folk Air. (F. W. B.)

Piano.

Key F. { .l₁ | l₁ .se₁ :l₁ .s₁ | l₁ :— .s₁ | l₁ .t₁ :d .r | m :— .m }
Lah is D.

Dear love, re-gard my grief, Do not my suit dis - dain; O

Pi - ty my griev-ous pain, Long suf-fer'd for thy sake, Do

{ m .,m :r .t₁ | l₁ .t₁ :d .r | m .,l₁ :l₁ .se₁ | l₁ :— .d | m .m :m .m }

yield me some re - lief____ That am with sor - row slain!

not my suit dis - dain,____ No time I rest can take,

These long sev'n years and

{ l :— .l | s .f :f .s | m :— .m | l .l :s .m | d .r :f .f }

more, Still have I lov'd thee; Do thou my joys res - tore,____ Fair

| m .d :l₁ | .,l₁ | l₁ :—.d | m .m :fe .se | l :m .m | r .,r :m .f |

la - dy pi - ty me, These long sev'n years and more,——Still have I lov - ed

| m :—.m | l₁ .,t₁ :d .r | m :—.r | m .l₁ :l₁ .se₁ | l₁ :—. |

thee; Do thou my joys res - tore, Fair la - dy, pi - ty me.

rall.

3
While that I live I love,
So fancy urgeth me;
My mind can not remove,
Such is my constancy.
My mind is nobly bent
Tho' I'm of low degree;
Sweet lady, give consent
To love and pity me.
These long seven years and more
Still have I loved thee;
Do thou my joys restore,
Fair lady, pity me.

THE STORM.

Words by STEPHENS.

Old English Air.
(W. H. H.)

Piano.

Key G.

Cease, rude Boreas, blust-'ring rail - er, List ye, lands-men all, to
Hark! the boat - swain hoarse-ly baw - ling, By top - sails and hal-yards

me; Mess - mates, hear a bro - ther sai - lor Sing the dan - gers of the
stand! Down top - gal - lants,quick, be haul - ing, Down your stay - sails, hand, boys

sea. From bounding bil - lows first in mo - tion,When the dis - tant whirl-winds
hand! How it fresh - ens! set the bra - ces, Quick! the top - sail sheets let

rise, To the tem - pest - troub - led o - cean, While the seas con - tend with
go; Luff, boys, luff, don't make wry fac - es, Up your top - sails nimb - ly

skies.
clew!

3

The foremast's gone! cries ev'ry tongue out,
  O'er the lee, twelve feet 'bove deck;
A leak beneath the chest-tree's sprung out,
  Call all hands to clear the wreck!
Guide the lanyards cut to pieces;
  Come my hearts, he stout and bold;
Plumb the well, the leak increases,
  Four feet water in the hold.

4

O'er the lee-beam lies the land, boys,
  Let the guns o'er-board be thrown;
To the pumps come ev'ry hand, boys,
  See! our mizzen-mast be gone.
The leak we've found, it cannot pour fast,
  We've lighten'd her a foot or more;
Up and rig a jury foremast;
  She rights! she rights, boys! wear off shore.

5

Now once more on joys we're thinking,
  Since kind fortune's spared our lives;
Come! the can, boys, let's be drinking
  To our sweethearts and our wives.
Fill it up, about ship wheel it;
  Close to th' lips a brimmer join;
Where's the tempest now? who feel it?
  None! our danger's drown'd in wine.

TELL ME WHERE IS FANCY BRED?

Words from SHAKESPEARE.

Sir JOHN STEVENSON. Mus. Doc.
(W. H. H.)

Allegretto staccato scherzando.

rall.   *p* *a tempo*

{ m .d:—| : | s :—|m:— d:—|—: | :d' |s :1 | m :f |d:— | — —:d' |s :1 | m :f |d:— 1:—| : }
gin it,   ding, dong bell,   ding ding ding ding dong bell,   ding ding ding ding dong bell; all,

a tempo

{ : | : | : | : | : |d' |s :1 |m :f | d :— | :d | s :f |m :f | d :— | :— f:—| : }
ding ding ding ding dong bell,   ding ding ding ding dong bell;   all,

p

    f   *dim.*   *p*

{ s:—| : | 1 :—|t:— d':—| : | 1:—| : s:—|:d' | r':—|t:— | d' :— |—:— |—:— |—:— | — :— |—:— }
all!   ding dong bell;   all,   all ding ding ding dong bell ____

    f

{ m:—| : | f :—'r :—|m:— : | f:—| : d:—|:s | f:—|r:— | m :— |—:—:d' |l :f |r :s | s :— | :d' }
all!   ding dong bell;   all,   all ding ding ding dong bell;   ding ding ding ding dong bell,   ding

8············

cres.   *dim.*   *rall.*   *pp*

{ : —: | —:— | — :—|—:— | —:— |—:— | —:— |—:— | —:— | — :— |—:—|—:— |—:—| : | : | :| : | }

cres.   *dim.*   *rall.*   *pp*

{ 1 :f |r :s | d :—|—:— |—:— | —:— | — :— |—:— | —:—|—:— | —:—|—:— | —:—| : | : | :| : | }
ding ding ding ding dong   bell. ____

dim.   *rall.*   *pp*

8

THE LASS OF THE MILL.

FESTING. (W. H. H.)

Key F.

| :d .r | m :r .d | s :f .m | l :t .d' | t :d' .t | d' :s .m | l :s .f |

Who has e'er been at Bal-dock must needs know the mill, At the sign of the Horse,at the

This man of the mill has a daugh-ter so fair, With so pleas-ing a shape,and so

| m :m .d | s :r .m | f :m .r | m .r :m .s | d' :t .l | se :l .t |

foot of the hill, Where the grave and the gay; the clown and the beau With-

win-ning an air That once, on the ev-er-green bank as she stood, I

3

But, looking again, I perceived my mistake,
For Venus tho' fair has the look of a rake,
While nothing but virtue and modesty fill
The more beautiful looks of the maid of the mill.

4

Since first I beheld this dear lass of the mill
I can ne'er be at rest, for, do what I will,
All the day and all night I sigh and think still
I shall die if deprived of the maid of the mill.

THE GALLANT SAILOR.

DUET.

With spirit.   *ten.*   Old English (F. W. B.)

Piano.

rall. poco

SOPRANO. *Nancy.*

Key A.

: |d :-.s₁ | l₁ :t₁ |d :s | f :m |r :-.d | s₁ :d |t₁ :l₁ | s₁ :- |d :s₁

Gal-lant sai-lor, oft you've told me, That you'd nev-er leave your love,   To your

TENOR.

|l₁ :t₁ |d :s | f :m |r :-.d | s₁ :d |t₁ :l₁ | s₁ :- |t₁ :r | s :-.d |f :-.f

vows I now must hold you, Now's the time your love to   prove.   Oft these ten-der arms con-

| f | :m | r :d | t₁ | :d | f :m | r :-|d | :r .m | f | :f₁ | r :m .fe | s | :s₁ | |
troll'd you, Do not now from me re - move; Oft these ten-der arms con - troll'd you,

: |s d | f :m | r ^{m r d r} :f .m | d : | | | :

Do not now from me re - move.

p

a tempo

p col. voce

f

Sailor.

| m :-.t₁ | d :r | m :l | s :f | m :-r | d ^m :r | d :-.t₁ | l₁ :- | d :-s₁ |
Is not Brit-ain's flag de - grad-ed? Have not French-men brav'd our fleet? How can

E. 4. g.

sai-lors live up - braid-ed, Not the Frenchmen dare to meet! What if Eng-land were in-

Nancy.

Hear me, gal-lant sai - lor, hear me, While our

vad-ed! Shall not we their in - so-lence beat! What if Eng-land were in-

col. voce   *a tempo*

coun-try has a foe,   He is mine, too, nev-er fear me, I may

Key E.

vad-ed, Shall not we their in - so-lence beat?   Is not Britains flag be-

THE RINGERS OF TORRINGTON TOWN.

Folk Song. (F. W. B.)

Key G.

1 Good ring-ers be we that in Tor-ring-ton dwell, And
2 The fifth is a doc-tor a man of re-nown, The

what that we are I will speed-i-ly tell,
Ten-or the Tail-or that clothes the whole town,

1. 2. 3. 4. 5. 6.

6. 5. 4. 3. 2. 1. One.

The first is call'd Tur-ner, the
The breez-es pro-claim in their

sec-ond call'd Swete, The third is a Vul-can, the fourth Har-ry Neat.
fall and their swell, No jar in the con-cord, no flaw in a bell.

1. 2. 3. 4. 5. 6. 6. 5. 4. 3. 2. 1. One.

rall.   poco

a tempo

3 The winds that are blowing on mountain and lea, Bear swiftly my message a - cross the blue sea,

1. 2. 3. 4. 5. 6.   6. 5. 4. 3. 2. 1.   One.   Stand

all men in or-der, give each man his due, We can't all be Tenors, but each can pull true,

1. 2. 3. 4. 5. 6.   6. 5. 4. 3. 2. 1.   One.

rall.

Sweet are the Charms of her I Love.

BARTON BOOTH.

R. LEVERIDGE.
(H. F. S.)

In moderate time and with expression.

Piano.

Lah is F.

Sweet are the charms of her I love, More fra - grant than the
True as the nee - dle to the pole, Or as the di - al

da - mask rose, Soft as the down of tur - tle dove,
to the sun, Constant as glid - ing wa - ters roll,

p rall.   tempo

Gen - tle as air when zephyr blows, Re - fresh - ing as de -
Whoso swel - ling tides o - bey the moon, From ev' - ry o - ther

scending rains, To sun-burnt climes and thirsty plains.
charmer free. My life and love shall fol-low thee.

3.

Devouring time with stealing pace,
  Makes lofty oaks and cedars bow,
And marble tow'rs and gates of brass
  In his rude march he levels low;
But time, destroying far and wide,
Love from the soul can ne'er divide.

4.

Love and his sister fair, the soul,
  Twin-born, from heaven together came;
Love will the universe control,
  When dying seasons lose their name;
Divine abodes shall own his power,
When time and death shall be no more.

BRUTUS.

Words by W. SMITH.

Music by W. BEALE.

When comes thy hour of tri - al nigh, Shalt
thou like hap - less Bru - tus sigh?
Shalt thou like hap - less Bru - tus sigh?

Maestoso.

Lah is D.
Shall hu - man ter - rors thy lone heart ap - pall? From thy be - night - ed

ff

trem.

HARES IN THE OLD PLANTATION.

Folk Song, (W. H. H.)

My fa-ther turn'd me out of doors, I'd no home nor ha-bi-ta-tion; I took my
O then I cros'd a field or two, With-out an-y hes-i-ta-tion, When up jump'd

dog, my gun and snares a-way to the old plan-ta-tion, I'll nev-er
one, a-way she ran, a-way to the old plan-ta-tion, When up jump'd

want a piece of bread with hares in the old plan-ta-tion.
one, a-way she ran, a-way to the old plan-ta-tion.

CHORUS.
Briskly.

Hares, hares, they run, they run; Af-ter them, hound! af-ter them, hound! Hares, hares, with dog and gun I'm in - de - pen - dent ev - er. 2ⁿᵈ time.

3

My dog he started after her
　Without my invitation,
He caught her by the back so small
　Just in the old plantation.
　　CHORUS. Hares, hares, &c.

4

Be mine a wild and wand'ring life
　As any in the nation,
Before a home and bairns and wife
　Give me hares in the old plantation.
　　CHORUS. Hares, hares, &c.

5

O I shall eat both bread and meat
　And drink in moderation,
Ne'er want a groat nor a good warm coat
　With hares in the old plantation.
　　CHORUS. Hares, hares, &c.

CEASE YOUR FUNNING.

Words (verse one) by GAY.

Air from "The Beggar's Opera" 1727.
(H. F. S.)

Gracefully, not too fast.

Piano.

Key F.

Cease your fun-ning,

Force or cun-ning Ne-ver shall my heart tre-pan; All these sal-lies

Are but ma-lice To se-duce my con-stant man.

2

As the dial,
Sans denial,
Answers to the solar ray,
As the flower
In the bower
Lives but in the sunny day;
Tho' you wheedle,
As the needle
Pointeth ever to the pole,
Such, my lover,
You'll discover
He is mine, in heart and soul.

E. 4. h.

O MOTHER, A HOOP!

Old English Air. (H. F. S.)

Key Ab.
Lah is F. What a fine thing I have seen to-day,

O mo-ther, a hoop! I must have one, and you can-not say, Nay,

O mo-ther, a hoop! For so I can trun-dle my hoop and can play, So

merry, so merry, and ever be gay, O mother, a plain wooden hoop!

O mother, a hoop!

2

What a fine thing I have seen to-day, O mother, a hoop!
I must have one and you cannot say, Nay, O mother, a hoop!
The ladies all wear it to set out the gown,
A hoop is the fashion, they tell me, in town,
    O mother, a plain hempen hoop!
       O mother, a hoop!

3

What a fine thing I have seen to-day, O mother, a hoop!
I must have one and you cannot say, Nay, O mother, a hoop!
A plain ring of gold turns a maid to a wife,
I must and I will have one, mother, 'odds life!
    O mother, a plain wedding hoop!
       O mother, a hoop!

THE MILLER'S WEDDING.

Old English. (W. H. H.)

Refrain which may be repeated in Chorus.

He loves Sue and Sue loves he, He loves Sue and Sue loves he;

While the wind blows and while the mill goes, Who'll be so hap-py, so hap-py as ye?

3

While Ralph he is able to work at the mill,
‖: And Sue is not shrewish, her tongue lieth still, :‖
Their joys will continue and ever be new,
‖: And none be so happy as Ralph and his Sue. :‖

4

Let folk of fine fashion be only agreed
‖: To marry for jointures, sign, sealing of deed; :‖
Such signing and sealing's no part of their bliss,
‖: Who settle their hearts and then seal with a kiss. :‖

FAIR SALLY.

Music by Dr M. GREENE
(F. W. B.)

Voice.

Piano.

Key Eb. | : .m :l .t | d' :-.t .l :se .l |
Lah is C. 1. Fair Sal-ly loved a bon-ny
3. Wel-come,she cry'd my con-stant

poco rit.

{ t .m : .f :m .d | d :-.l.l:d .r | m : .m :l .t | d' :-.t .l :t .d' }
sea-man, With tears she sent him out to roam; Young Thomas lov'd no other
Tho-mas, Tho' out of sight, ne'er out of mind; Our hearts,tho' seas have parted

Key A♭.
Lah is F.

| wo-man But left his heart | with her at home. | She view'd the sea | from off the |
| from us, Yet they my thoughts | did leave be - hind. | So much did fan - | cy take thy |

Key E♭.
Lah is C.

ad lib.

| hill, And while she | turn'd the spin - ning wheel, | | Sung of her bon - ny |
| part, That time nor | ab - sence from my heart, | | Could drive my bon - ny |

sea - man.
Tho-mas.

2. The winds blew loud   and she grew paler,   To see the wea - ther cock turn
4. This thim-ble didst   thou give to Sally,   When this I see   I think of

round. When lo! she spy'd her bon- ny sai-lor Come whistling o'er the fal-low
you. Then why does Tom stand shilly shally, With yon-der stee - ple clear in

ground; With nim- ble feet she leap'd the stile Sweet Sal- ly met him with a
view! Tom, ne - ver to oc-ca- sion blind, Now took her in the com ing

smile, And kiss'd her bon- ny sai- lor.
mind And went to church with Sal - ly.

poco rit.

Fine.